Dream of
the Blue Turtle

★ Also by ★
Debbie Dadey

MERMAID TALES

Coming Soon

Mermaid Tales

★ Debbie Dadey ★

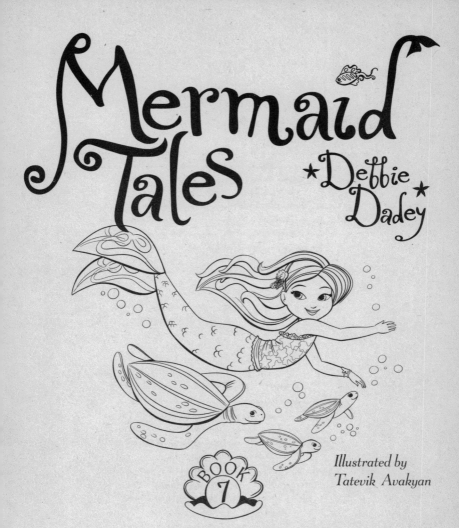

Illustrated by
Tatevik Avakyan

BOOK 7

Dream of the Blue Turtle

ALADDIN

NEW YORK   LONDON   TORONTO   SYDNEY   NEW DELHI

This book is a work of fiction. Any references to historical events, real people,
or real places are used fictitiously. Other names, characters, places, and events
are products of the author's imagination, and any resemblance to actual events
or places or persons, living or dead, is entirely coincidental.

ALADDIN

An imprint of Simon & Schuster Children's Publishing Division

1230 Avenue of the Americas, New York, NY 10020

First Aladdin paperback edition January 2014

Text copyright © 2014 by Debbie Dadey

Illustrations copyright © 2014 by Tatevik Avakyan

All rights reserved, including the right of reproduction in whole or in part in any form.

ALADDIN is a trademark of Simon & Schuster, Inc.,

and related logo is a registered trademark of Simon & Schuster, Inc.

Also available in an Aladdin hardcover edition.

For information about special discounts for bulk purchases,

please contact Simon & Schuster Special Sales at 1-866-506-1949

or business@simonandschuster.com.

The Simon & Schuster Speakers Bureau can bring authors to your live event.

For more information or to book an event contact the

Simon & Schuster Speakers Bureau at 1-866-248-3049

or visit our website at www.simonspeakers.com.

Book design by Karin Paprocki

The text of this book was set in Belucian Book.

Manufactured in the United States of America 1213 OFF

2 4 6 8 10 9 7 5 3 1

Library of Congress Control Number 2013943924

ISBN 978-1-4424-8264-7 (hc)

ISBN 978-1-4424-8263-0 (pbk)

ISBN 978-1-4424-8265-4 (eBook)

To Mary Jo and Fred
at Fredsusedwebsites.com.
Thanks for all your help!

* * * *

Thanks to awesome editors Karen Nagel
and Amy Cloud.

Cast of Characters

Shelly

Echo

Kiki

Pearl

Rocky

Contents

Leatherback Turtles

MRS. KARP, ARE YOU *sure* that is safe?" Pearl Swamp asked her third-grade teacher. Kiki Coral and the rest of the class waited for the reply.

"Of course," Mrs. Karp said, raising one green eyebrow as she responded to Pearl. "I wouldn't have asked a leatherback turtle to visit our school on Thursday if there was any danger."

"But aren't they awfully big?" Kiki asked. Her friends Shelly Siren and Echo Reef glanced at her. Kiki was one of the smallest mergirls at Trident Academy. She had been scared of whales because of their huge size.

Mrs. Karp nodded. "Yes, Kiki. Leatherbacks can weigh up to two thousand pounds and be seven feet long."

"And it's coming into *our* classroom?" Pearl said with her green eyes wide. "What if it sits on one of us?"

"We'd have smashed Pearl jam!" Rocky Ridge teased.

Several merstudents squealed until Mrs. Karp reassured them. "Marvin will not be in the classroom. We will meet him in the front hallway of the school, where there is plenty of room. Before we meet, I want you to prepare one or two questions to ask him."

"Marvin?" Rocky yelled. "What kind of turtle is named Marvin?"

"A very big one," Kiki said softly. Kiki knew leatherbacks weren't as large as whales, but something made her feel uncomfortable. She didn't know why.

"Marvin is a lovely name," Mrs. Karp told them. "Just as nice as Rockwell."

"Rockwell?" Pearl giggled. "Who is named Rockwell?"

"Nobody," Rocky said, but his cheeks were bright red.

Mrs. Karp continued. "Leatherbacks are the largest turtles in the ocean, class. They breathe air, so they can't stay underwater too long. They feed mostly on jellyfish."

"How do they get so big by eating just jellyfish, Mrs. Karp?" Shelly asked.

"Jellyfish are made up of almost all water."

"It's a bit of a mystery," Mrs. Karp agreed.

"Maybe the mystery is that they eat mergirls, too," Rocky said with a laugh. This caused Pearl and several other mergirls to shriek in fear. Shelly just rolled her eyes at Rocky. He was always telling bad jokes.

"That will be enough out of you, Rocky Ridge," Mrs. Karp said with a slap of her white tail on her marble desk.

Mrs. Karp went on to tell the merclass that leatherback turtles were endangered. "Floating plastic bags look very much like jellyfish. Sadly, the turtles don't realize their mistake until they've eaten the trash. If they eat too many bags, they can die."

Most of the third graders listened to every word, but Kiki barely heard her teacher. Her eyes grew cloudy and her ears stopped up. She knew what was happening. She was having one of her visions.

Kiki covered her face with her hands. In her mind she saw a frightening sight: Rocky Ridge, an enormous leatherback, and swirling water! Suddenly she shouted, "Mrs. Karp! I have to go see Madame Hippocampus! Now!"

The whole classroom stared at Kiki. "What is the meaning of this outburst?" Mrs. Karp asked.

Kiki twisted her hands together. She looked down at her purple tail. "I'm sorry. It's just that I need to see Madame right away." After what she had seen, Kiki desperately needed the advice of their merology teacher.

Mrs. Karp shook her head. "That is impossible. She is ill today."

Kiki gulped. What was she going to do? This couldn't wait. Not one more merminute.

Mr. Fangtooth

DO YOU SEE THAT?" SHELLY asked Kiki and Echo. "Mr. Fangtooth is smiling!"

The mergirls looked up from their lunch table to stare at the cafeteria worker. Mr. Fangtooth was usually very grouchy. Since the beginning of the school year, the three friends had tried to cheer him up. Once they had made funny faces. Another time they'd made silly noises. One day they'd told jokes. Nothing had worked. But today Mr. Fangtooth smiled and even whistled a cheerful tune as he cleaned tables and served food to the merkids.

Echo giggled. "I think he's happy. I bet he got back together with Lillian, his old sweetheart."

Shelly tossed a piece of seaweed called sailor's eyeball up in the water and caught it in her mouth. "I saw Mr. Fangtooth with Lillian yesterday at my Shell Wars game. They were holding hands!"

"It's so romantic!" Echo said with a giggle. She sipped her seaweed juice before saying, "Shelly, you were totally wavy yesterday. I cheered so hard when you made the winning goal."

"It was so exciting," Shelly said. "I thought for sure the Poseidon Prep School's octopus would block my shot. Did you see it, Kiki?"

But Kiki didn't answer. She was staring into a dark corner of the lunchroom. Her sea grapes sat untouched in front of her. "Kiki!" Echo said sharply. "What's wrong with you? Didn't you hear Shelly?"

Kiki jumped and asked, "What makes you think something is wrong?"

"Ever since Mrs. Karp told us about a

leatherback turtle visiting us, you've been acting really funny," Shelly told her. "Are you afraid of leatherbacks because they're so big—just like with the whales?"

"At first I was," Kiki answered. "But I'm not afraid. I like leatherbacks. My dad even taught me to speak their language."

"Sweet seaweed," Shelly said. "Can you teach us a few words?"

"Maybe later," Kiki said. She knew Shelly loved ocean languages, but right now Kiki couldn't think about teaching anyone anything. She grabbed her tray and sped away from the table.

"Where are you going?" Echo called after her.

"I . . . I'm not hungry," Kiki said, looking

 11

back at Echo. Kiki didn't know what to do. She had never told her friends about her special dreams, or visions, of the future. Usually the dreams were good, but every once in a while they were scary. The one she'd had this morning had been horrible, especially for Rocky!

Kiki needed to speak to a merology expert like Madame Hippocampus desperately. Madame would know what Kiki's vision meant and what she should do. But what if Madame was out of school the rest of the week? Would it be too late for Rocky?

As Kiki rushed away, she bumped into another lunch table. Her salad of sea grapes and sea lettuce splattered all over

the Neptune, King of the Sea statue. A big blob of lettuce sat on his head like a slimy green hat.

"Oh my Neptune!" Pearl screeched from across the cafeteria. "Look what Kiki did!" It took only a second for Rocky to point and laugh. Pretty soon half of the merkids in the cafeteria were snickering at Kiki's accident.

"Echo, look," Shelly said, nodding at Mr. Fangtooth. He wasn't whistling anymore. And he wasn't smiling. He was swimming toward Kiki with a frown on his face.

"We have to help Kiki before Mr. Fangtooth gets to her!" Echo squealed. "And then we have to find out what's really wrong with her."

Kiki's Gift

SHELLY BRAVELY SWISHED IN front of Mr. Fangtooth as he swam toward Kiki. "Don't worry, sir," Shelly told him. "We'll clean up the mess."

"It was an accident," Echo added.

Mr. Fangtooth grunted and floated

away, acting like his usual crabby self. Quick as a bubble, Echo and Shelly grabbed two cleaner wrasse from the kitchen service counter. They held the fish next to the statue so the wrasse could eat the lettuce.

Kiki reached for a grape that had rolled to the back of the statue. "I've almost got it," she said, stretching her arm as far as she could. Just as she touched the sea grape, she felt something grab her hair and pull it hard.

"Aaah!" Kiki squealed. "Save me! I'm stuck!"

Shelly and Echo came to Kiki's rescue. Her long black hair was caught on Neptune's trident. "Wow, Kiki," Echo said.

"It's really tangled." Together, Echo and Shelly pulled Kiki's hair free.

Kiki rubbed her sore head. "I wish this was the worst of it."

"What do you mean?" Echo asked. "What's going on?"

Kiki glanced around the cafeteria. No one was looking their way anymore, but she still wasn't certain that she should tell Echo and Shelly about her gift and what she had seen.

Kiki had to be sure no other merkids overheard her, so she pulled her friends out to the play yard. No one was supposed to be out there yet, so it was deserted. Kiki gently tapped a sea-squirt ball with a purple tail fin.

Suddenly Kiki was worried. Maybe she should keep her visions a secret. Would Shelly and Echo think she was weird? But then Kiki thought about what good friends the mergirls had been to her. After all, when Pearl had gotten Kiki thrown

out of her dorm room, Shelly and Echo had helped her move. They had also supported her when she'd been scared of the whales. Maybe they could help now.

Finally Kiki said, "Before I tell you anything, you have to promise not to tell anyone."

"Tell anyone what?" Shelly asked.

"Seal swear?" Kiki asked, looking from Shelly's blue eyes to Echo's dark brown ones.

Both girls repeated the merkid promise: "Seal swear."

Kiki took a deep breath. "You know how Madame Hippocampus said some merfolk can see the future?" Kiki said.

Echo nodded.

Kiki whispered, "I can do that."

"What? We can't hear you. Speak louder," Shelly said.

Kiki splashed the water with her purple tail. "I can see the future. I have visions."

"No wavy way," Echo said. "Since when?"

Kiki shrugged. "I don't have them all the time, but I've had them for as long as I can remember."

"Can your seventeen brothers do it too?" Shelly asked. "What about your mom and dad?"

Kiki shook her head. "I don't think so."

Echo giggled. "That's so cool. I thought you were going to tell us something bad."

"You don't understand," Kiki said. "I've seen the future, and it's horrible!"

Turtle Shell

THE NEXT DAY BEFORE school, Shelly and Echo begged Kiki to tell them more about what she had seen and why it upset her. But Kiki wouldn't say a word.

Later, when swimming past the library,

Shelly asked, "What did you see?" But Kiki still wouldn't tell her.

And during art class in the back of the room, Echo said, "Tell us what you saw!" But Kiki kept her mouth closed tight.

When it was storytelling class, Echo whispered, "What was your vision about? You can't keep a secret forever."

Kiki shook her head. "I want to tell you, but I really have to talk to Madame first to make sure what I saw was real." After her vision yesterday, she hadn't had any more. *Maybe it was nothing after all,* she thought.

But during science class, Kiki was reminded of her dangerous dream. Mrs. Karp talked about the many different types of turtles in the ocean. She displayed several types of turtle shells. "Which one of these belongs to the leatherback?" she asked.

Rocky's hand shot up. He blurted out, "The biggest one!"

"Good guess," Mrs. Karp said, "but it's not the answer I'm looking for."

The smile on Rocky's face disappeared as Mrs. Karp explained, "That was a trick question because leatherbacks don't actually have a hard shell."

"That wasn't fair, Mrs. Karp," Rocky's friend Adam complained.

Then Shelly raised her

hand. "But I thought *all* turtles had shells."

Mrs. Karp smiled. "Actually, the leatherback's carapace is rubbery, with no hard plates," their teacher explained. And then she continued, "The leatherback turtle has been in the ocean for one hundred million years."

"That's older than Madame Hippocampus," Pearl said with a snicker. Kiki's heart fluttered. Madame Hippocampus was still out sick today and Kiki was running out of time. Melvin's visit was in a few more days. How much longer was she going to have to wait to ask about her vision?

"Of course, our friend Marvin isn't that old," Mrs. Karp said. "But Marvin's ancestors were here many millions of years ago. And now it's time to learn about your next assignment."

"Oh no," Echo said, before slapping her hand over her mouth. Kiki felt the same way. Mrs. Karp was always giving their class lots of homework and reports. Since the beginning of the school year they had sculpted mollusks, caught shrimp and krill, dived with humpback whales, and even learned about merfolk's biggest enemy, the shark. What was their green-haired teacher going to ask them to do next?

"This lesson is designed to encourage creativity and build cooperative skills," Mrs. Karp told them.

The merstudents muttered. What was Mrs. Karp talking about?

Shelly raised her hand. "Does that mean we'll work with someone else?"

Mrs. Karp nodded. If Kiki had to have a partner, she hoped it would be Shelly or Echo. But maybe Kiki should ask to work with Rocky, just in case she had to make sure he was safe. Her vision had to do with Rocky, after all.

Kiki looked around the room at the merstudents. She stared at Pearl's pearl necklace and glittery shirt. Kiki sure hoped she didn't have to work with Pearl. Something about her rubbed Kiki the wrong way. Pearl seemed to think she was better than everyone else.

Mrs. Karp went on. "Since leatherback turtles don't have a regular shell, I'd like you to design a fun kind of house for them."

"How about a clown-fish house?" Rocky teased. "Clowns are fun."

"Use your imaginations," Mrs. Karp continued. "I expect you and your partner to be creative and original. This project will allow you to use math skills, such as measuring and shapes. You can show your artistic sides. And you'll have a chance to learn how to be part of a team."

"Will we be building the houses in art class?" Adam asked.

Mrs. Karp answered, "No, Adam. This is a homework assignment. But because of our classroom's limited size, you should make your pretend house small enough to fit on the top of your desk. Your houses are due by the end of the week."

Kiki usually liked schoolwork, and this task sounded more fun than most. Now she just hoped for a good partner. She crossed her purple tail fins as Mrs. Karp began calling out names.

"Shelly, you may work with Wanda. Rocky and Echo, you are partners," Mrs. Karp said.

Kiki could hear Echo's gasp. She felt a little sorry for Echo because Rocky was a bit of a goof-off. But when Mrs. Karp announced, "Pearl and Kiki, you are a team," she felt equally sorry for herself.

Worst Luck

I STILL DON'T KNOW WHAT TO DO! This has been the worst day ever," Kiki told Echo and Shelly after the conch shell sounded to end the school day. They were standing in the enormous entrance hall to Trident Academy. The shell ceiling was filled with colorful carvings of famous merpeople. A gigantic chandelier of glowing jellyfish lit up the large gathering spot. The hall was big enough to fit a humpback whale. Kiki shivered when she thought about the leatherback turtle that would be there on Thursday.

Merkids from third through tenth grade floated past them, some to the school dorms and others to their homes. Kiki's family lived far away in the eastern oceans, so she lived in the Trident Academy girls' dormitory. Shelly and Echo lived with their families only a short swim away in Trident City.

"I know what will cheer you up," Echo said. "Come with us and we'll treat you to some seaweed juice at the Big Rock Café."

"That's a great idea," Shelly said, tugging

Kiki toward the door. "You'll feel much better."

In less than ten tail shakes, the three mergirls sat in a booth near the front of the café. Lots of other students from Trident Academy talked and laughed at nearby tables.

Kiki choked on her green juice and ducked under the stone table. Pearl was headed their way! "Don't tell her I'm here," Kiki begged.

"Have you seen Kiki?" Pearl asked. "I thought we could start on our turtle house. She is so lucky to have me for a partner."

"Isn't she in her dorm room?" Shelly asked innocently.

Pearl frowned. "No."

"Do you want some seaweed juice?" Echo said, raising her shell cup toward Pearl. Kiki squeezed Echo's pink tail.

Pearl sniffed the water. "No, I guess I'll just go home." The girls watched Pearl swim out of the restaurant.

"I can't believe you asked her to have juice with you," Kiki said, sliding up from underneath the table.

Echo shrugged. "I knew she'd say no. She's not very friendly."

"You guys are the best. You'd do anything for me," Kiki said. And at that moment, she absolutely knew she could trust Shelly and Echo.

"I want to tell you about my vision," Kiki said.

Shelly put her arm around Kiki. "We're your buddies, Kiki. We want to help you. You can trust us."

Kiki felt a tear at the corner of her eye. It meant so much to her that Shelly and Echo were her friends, especially since her own family lived so far away. Kiki thought about the little orange starfish her mermom had given her before she left for Trident Academy. She wished she had it with her now since it brought her good luck and made her feel more confident. Instead it was back in her dorm room, hidden under her pillow.

"The problem is," Kiki said, "I only see flashes of the future. Yesterday, I saw something that really frightened me. There was swirling water, Rocky screaming, and a big turtle falling toward him."

Shelly and Echo glanced at each other. "What do you think it means?" Echo asked.

"That's the trouble," Kiki said. "I don't know. It sure didn't look good, and it gave me a terrible feeling."

Then Shelly spoke. "It doesn't have to be something bad. Maybe Rocky and Marvin were playing hide-and-seek or tag? My grandfather says, 'Don't borrow trouble,'" she said, taking a sip of her seaweed juice. "That means don't worry about something that might be nothing."

"Maybe you're right," Kiki answered. But she still couldn't help being worried, even though Shelly's grandfather Siren was a very wise merman.

As the three mergirls finished their snacks, Kiki saw Mr. Fangtooth float by the café. "Look!" She pointed. Unfortunately, her arm bumped her juice and it spilled all over the table.

"Let's see if he's meeting his sweetheart," Echo suggested. "Then we'll know if that's why he was so happy yesterday."

The friends quickly cleaned up the mess and hurried outside to follow Mr. Fangtooth. "I think he's going in the direction of the Manta Ray Express Station," Echo said. "Let's go!"

"Oh my goodness," Shelly said. "Look at that." The girls giggled as Mr. Fangtooth hugged a merlady they recognized as Lillian.

"Isn't that sweet?" Echo said. "They *are* back together."

"Why couldn't I have a vision about something nice like that?" Kiki said.

Happy with their discovery, the girls started to go home, but Kiki heard Pearl's voice calling her. "Kiki! Kiki! Where are you going? We have to get started on our turtle house. I have such wonderful ideas! We'll build the *best* one in class. It's going to be so fun!"

Kiki wanted to groan, but she knew it would be rude. She wanted to swim away, but she knew it would be impolite. And they did have to get their homework done.

Kiki didn't have a choice about doing

her project with Pearl. But if Madame wasn't back in school by tomorrow, Kiki would have to come up with another plan to save Rocky—if her vision was as bad as she believed it was.

6

Teamwork?

LET'S GO TO THE CRAFT ROOM," Pearl suggested as the two mergirls entered Pearl's huge shell.

"You have a room just for crafts?" Kiki asked.

Pearl giggled and twisted her long strand of pearls. "Sure, we have a room for just about everything. One for dancing. One for music. One for books. One for . . ."

"I get it," Kiki said. Because of her seventeen brothers, Kiki's home didn't have any extra space. In fact, she was the only one who had a bedroom to herself. Her brothers were jealous because they shared rooms, but when she had visions late at night, she wished she shared a room with one of them. She had kept her gift a secret from everyone in her family. Of course, she'd never seen anything so scary before.

Pearl floated up the fancy staircase and into a big room that had long stone countertops filled with bottles and trunks. Every shelf was overflowing with colorful shells, beads, and ribbons. "My mermom loves to craft," Pearl explained. "But we can use any of this stuff."

"Wow!" Kiki exclaimed.

"Now," Pearl said, facing Kiki. "Let's just get this straight from the beginning. We're using my materials, so *I'm* in charge and we're going to do it my way." Pearl pushed back her headband and tapped her gold tail on the polished marble floor. The look on her face said she was ready to argue if Kiki didn't agree.

Pearl's actions were giving Kiki a head-ache. She wanted to protest and tell Pearl that Mrs. Karp had said they needed to work together. They were supposed to be a team. Kiki wanted to share the great ideas that she had, but she didn't think Pearl would listen, and she didn't want to get into a fight. After all, she was still worried about her vision and what might happen to Rocky, and now her head ached, too, so she just said, "Okay."

It only took a merminute for Kiki to regret agreeing. "These colorful bags are perfect for a turtle house," Pearl suggested, putting a large container of them on the counter.

"But those bags are made of plastic. Mrs. Karp said those are bad for leatherbacks," Kiki said.

"Oh barnacles! We're just making a house," Pearl said. "We're not hurting anything."

Kiki sighed and rubbed her aching head. "But I think we should make the turtle house out of something else."

"My house. My rules," Pearl snapped. "Why don't you get started and I'll go get us a snack?" She floated out of the room.

A merhour later, Kiki had finished the turtle house and Pearl still hadn't come back. Kiki was more than a little mad. She may not have known what was going to happen with Rocky, but she was right about Pearl being her homework partner: It wasn't one little bit fun.

Madame's Advice

KIKI WOKE UP EARLY THE NEXT morning. She lay quietly in her killer whale skeleton bed, and when she stretched, a gray heron feather tickled her nose. Under her pillow she felt her lucky starfish charm. But the quiet feeling didn't last for long—suddenly she remembered her vision and quickly got out of bed. She needed to talk to Madame Hippocampus as soon as possible! Hopefully, she was well today and back at school.

Marvin was coming tomorrow and Kiki knew she had to find out what her vision meant before the leatherback came to their school.

Kiki zoomed out of the girls' dormitory and headed to the main entrance hall of Trident Academy. A few other early risers were already there, chatting in the enormous open room. Two merboys were using the time to play porcupine fish bowling. Kiki was sure Headmaster Hermit wouldn't approve.

"Kiki!" Shelly called to her and waved.

To Kiki's dismay, Shelly and Echo had also come to school early, and they swam over to join her. This was one morning when Kiki didn't want to talk to her friends. She just wanted to see Madame. "Hi!" Kiki said.

"How was working with Pearl?" Echo asked.

"She made me do all the work!" Kiki complained. "And she wanted to use plastic bags for the turtle's house!"

Shelly scrunched her nose and said, "You're kidding. But that sounds like Pearl. Wanda and I had lots of fun on our project. She has great ideas."

Echo nodded. "Even Rocky helped me.

We worked last night at my shell." Then she giggled. "It was hard to concentrate on the project because he's so cute. He wouldn't stop telling jokes."

"I hope you didn't tell him about my vision," said Kiki.

"There's really not much to say. You only saw flashes and we don't know what they mean," Echo said.

Shelly nodded and said, "But you really should tell Mrs. Karp about Pearl not helping."

Kiki couldn't even think about Pearl right now. She had to talk to Madame Hippocampus before school started. Even though she had told Shelly and Echo how worried she was, they didn't understand how serious the vision was. "Maybe later," Kiki said. "Right now I have to see Madame."

"We'll go with you," Echo said. Kiki started to argue, but she was worried about running out of time before school began, so she zipped off, with Shelly and Echo racing behind her.

Madame Hippocampus's room was to the right of the main hall, past the library. Kiki zoomed through the door and almost hugged Madame Hippocampus. "Madame! I'm so glad you're here!" Kiki said. "I need to talk to you. It's a life-or-death situation!"

"Well, goodness. Come right in, mer-ladies!" Madame said, tapping a hoof on her marble desk. By now the girls were used to their merology teacher's unusual appearance. She had a horse face, hooves, and the plump lower end of a dolphin.

Kiki's heart was beating so fast, she thought it would explode. She took a couple of deep breaths and then began. "Madame, I had a vision. I've had them before, but never

this scary. And other than Shelly and Echo, I've never told anyone." Kiki stopped for a second and said, "The other day I saw Rocky screaming and a huge turtle falling toward him."

Madame was silent, and then a huge smile showed all of her horse teeth. "That is very interesting, Kiki. You may not be happy about what you saw with Marvin and Rocky, but you are a very fortunate young mermaid."

"That's what we told her," Echo said.

Kiki shook her head sadly. "I don't feel fortunate. And neither will Rocky, if what I saw comes true!"

Madame floated over and patted Kiki's

shoulder. "My dear, only a few merfolk have this gift. You are special."

"It's not special," Kiki said, almost in tears. "It's awful. I don't know what's going to happen, but I felt like it was bad."

Suddenly Kiki wiped away her tears. "Madame, I just thought of something. Can the future be changed?" she asked.

Madame nodded. "A fine question, Kiki. Well, since it's the future, it hasn't happened yet. I would say yes."

For the first time since her vision, Kiki felt better. She had an idea and hoped it would save Rocky's life and prove her vision wrong.

T-day

FTER THE THREE MERGIRLS left Madame Hippocampus's room, they floated down the hallway to their own third-grade class. Luckily, only a few kids were in their seats already. "Mrs. Karp," Kiki exclaimed, "I must speak to you. You have to cancel the leatherback's visit."

Mrs. Karp looked up from her seaweed book and frowned. "Why do you say that, Kiki? We have been planning this event with Marvin for a while."

"But . . . I . . ." Kiki didn't know what to say. More merkids were coming into class. Was she going to have to tell Mrs. Karp about her horrible vision in front of the other third graders and frighten everyone?

Kiki held her head up and straightened her back. She had to do it. She opened her mouth, but at that moment, a mergirl named Morgan swished past her to complain to

Mrs. Karp. "Adam isn't helping me one bit with the turtle house project."

Mrs. Karp raised a green eyebrow at Adam. "Excuse me, Kiki. One moment," she said. She turned to Adam. "Is this true?"

Adam frowned. "No, Morgan is being pushy. She wants to make the whole house out of pink coral. I hate pink!" Kiki noticed most of the desks were filled with merkids now. Pearl was in her seat. This would be the perfect time to tell Mrs. Karp how Pearl hadn't helped either and how she wanted to use plastic bags that endangered the turtles.

But before Kiki could say anything, Mrs. Karp spoke to the entire classroom.

"Keep in mind that no matter what you do in this ocean, you will have to work with other merpeople. Some will not be very cooperative." Mrs. Karp paused to glance at Adam and then Pearl.

Kiki was surprised. Did Mrs. Karp know that Pearl didn't help? Pearl glared at Kiki. Did Pearl think Kiki had told on her?

Mrs. Karp continued. "Remember that part of this lesson is to learn how to work together."

Kiki sighed. It didn't look like Mrs. Karp was going to change tomorrow's plans.

Rocky floated into the room just as Mrs. Karp finished talking to the class.

"Echo and I are making the best turtle house ever," he bragged.

Kiki looked at Rocky. She wasn't sure why Echo thought he was cute, but she didn't want anything to happen to him and knew she couldn't give up. She had to come up with another plan, and maybe Rocky had to be a part of it.

At recess, Kiki swam up to where Rocky was swinging from a tube sponge. She said, "Rocky, you can't come to school tomorrow."

He swung to the ocean floor and grinned. "Now, that's what I've been waiting to hear all year."

Kiki smiled. She never dreamed keeping Rocky away from Trident Academy would be that easy. Her problem was solved.

But then Rocky folded his arms across his chest and scratched his nose with his brown tail. "I have just one question, Kiki. *Why* can't I come to school tomorrow?" he asked.

Kiki frowned. "Because . . ." She tried to think of a good reason. She didn't want to tell Rocky that she could see the future—his future—and that he was in danger. Couldn't he just stay home and enjoy it?

Then Rocky said, "Hey, that big leatherback is supposed to come tomorrow. I don't want to miss T-day!"

"T-day?" Kiki asked.

"Yeah," Rocky said, jumping back on the tube sponge and swinging his tail around. "Turtle day!"

Kiki groaned. Now what was she going to do?

Library

AFTER RECESS, KIKI SAT IN the Trident Academy library next to Shelly and Echo. Kiki didn't notice the gleaming mother-of-pearl domed ceiling. She didn't pay attention to the fancy chandeliers that had been saved from a sunken ship or the fact that they glowed with the bioluminescent light of mauve stinger jellyfish. She was supposed to be looking in the stacks of seaweed books for information about leatherback turtles for her questions for Marvin, but she was having trouble concentrating.

She kept staring at Rocky. He was busy throwing little pebbles at Pearl when her back was turned. Whenever Pearl looked at Rocky, he glanced at his seaweed papers like he was studying hard.

"Did you already think of a good interview question?" Shelly asked her.

Kiki squealed. Everyone in the library turned to look at her. The librarian, Miss

Scylla, frowned but continued helping Morgan with her book.

"Sorry," Shelly whispered. "I didn't mean to startle you."

Kiki managed a small smile. "That's okay. What are you talking about? What interview question?"

Shelly's red hair floated in the water around her. "That's what we're supposed to be doing—trying to figure out a good question to ask Marvin tomorrow."

Kiki's throat tightened. She was running out of time. Kiki grabbed Shelly's arm and whispered, "You have to help me stop Marvin from visiting."

Echo put her hand over her heart. "Do

you think we should warn Rocky, just in case?" Echo said.

Kiki nodded. Maybe Echo was finally realizing how serious the vision had been. "I tried to stop Rocky from coming today, but he wouldn't listen to me. Maybe the three of us can change his mind."

"Come on," Echo said.

Shelly said, "I don't know if that's such a good idea. . . ." But Echo was already halfway across the library.

Kiki sped after Echo. She had to make sure Echo didn't tell Rocky the whole truth. If Rocky knew about Kiki's visions, he'd never stop making fun of her. Why did she have to have a special gift like this? Why couldn't her gift be to sing nicely like Shelly or twist and do flips like Echo?

As the mergirls swam over to Rocky, Pearl grew tired of Rocky's teasing and pushed him toward Echo. Rocky fell into Echo, who tumbled onto Kiki, who crashed into Shelly. They all toppled over into a large rock shelf loaded with seaweed books. The books crashed onto the library floor, covering the four merkids.

Kiki popped her head up from the mess and saw Miss Scylla heading their way.

LATER THAT NIGHT, KIKI WAS AS WORRIED as ever that she couldn't put a stop to

tomorrow's disaster. They had never had a chance to warn Rocky. After their library pileup, Miss Scylla had made them tidy up and then sent them home.

Tomorrow was coming, like it or not. And there was nothing Kiki could do to change it.

Polka Dots?

KIKI COULDN'T STOP HER purple tail from shaking and shaking. It was the next morning and she was in her classroom waiting for Marvin to arrive.

Mrs. Karp smiled at her merstudents. "Good morning, class. This is an exciting day for us. Let's review proper behavior. No one will interrupt our guest. No one will speak unless called upon. There will be no chatting among students and absolutely no loud noises. We don't want to upset our guest.

"We will show Marvin how well-behaved Trident Academy students can be. If not, there will be consequences."

Adam raised a tail fin. "What's 'consequences'?"

"Consequences are what will happen to you if you do not follow the rules," Mrs. Karp said, glaring over her tiny glasses.

Kiki looked at Rocky and Adam. They didn't ask anything else about consequences. No one wanted to find out what they would be. They'd gotten in enough trouble yesterday in the library. Mrs. Karp had been so upset that she'd threatened to cancel Marvin's visit, but then she said it wouldn't be fair to Marvin, so he was still coming.

Kiki was so tired she could hardly think. All evening and into the night, she had tried to figure out what else to do to save Rocky. Mrs. Karp wouldn't cancel the visit. Rocky wouldn't stay home. Madame thought Kiki's vision was a gift. Even Shelly and Echo didn't think her vision was really all that dangerous.

When Mrs. Karp asked the class to line up, Kiki found herself at the end of the line with Rocky. All of a sudden she whispered, "Rocky, Mrs. Karp has a special job just for you. She wants you to go to Mr. Fangtooth's office. There is a present for Marvin there. And you'll get to give it to him."

Rocky's face lit up and he grinned. When the class floated out the door toward the front hall, Rocky floated in the opposite direction. Kiki couldn't believe it. She had worried for no reason. It had been so easy to get Rocky away from Marvin. She felt terrible about telling a lie. But she felt wonderful for saving Rocky. Hopefully, by the time Rocky found out there wasn't a present, Marvin would already be gone. After all, turtles couldn't stay underwater for long. Kiki was relieved.

She got to the entrance hall just as Marvin arrived.

Wow! He was gigantic! His body took up the whole door and his flippers glided him directly underneath the glittering, glowing jellyfish chandelier.

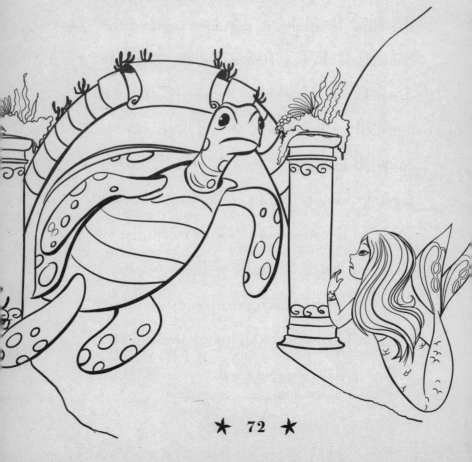

"Oh my gosh," Pearl said, giggling. "He has pink spots!"

Mrs. Karp gave Pearl a stern look. Kiki had to admit she hadn't expected the leatherback to be covered with pink and white polka dots. It was kind of cheerful.

But Marvin's face wasn't friendly at all. In fact, he looked downright mean.

11

Too Loud!

ECHO AND SHELLY SWAM OVER to Kiki's side. "Where's Rocky?" Echo asked, her eyes wide.

"Shhh," Kiki whispered. "I sent him on a wild eel chase."

"Good work, Kiki," Shelly said. "Maybe you did change the future."

Just then Mrs. Karp frowned at them. The mergirls got quiet. They turned their attention to Marvin, whose round body filled the center of the huge hallway. The leatherback stood on his back flippers, his head almost touching the enormous golden entrance hall chandelier. Shining jellyfish on the fixture lit up the large room.

Marvin was big and he looked mean, but when he opened his mouth he didn't sound scary at all. He seemed really nice!

"Hello, merboys and mergirls," Marvin said in perfect merfolk speech. "It is quite a pleasure to be with you today. I love visiting your delightful school and, of course, your teacher."

Marvin continued, "I can't stay underwater too long, but I'll happily answer any questions you might have about leatherback turtles and my travels."

It turned out that Marvin had been almost everywhere in the oceans with his friend Sheldon. Kiki felt bad when Marvin told them how his good friend had almost died from eating plastic bags. She decided if she ever saw a plastic bag floating in the water, she'd grab it so no other turtles would die. She was angry with Pearl for making her build a house out of them. And Kiki was mad at herself for allowing Pearl to force her. Although, maybe using them for other things was better than letting them float in the ocean.

"Wh-where are your favorite waters?" Morgan asked.

"The Sea of Japan is quite lovely this time of year," Marvin told the merclass. Kiki smiled because that was near where her family lived. She was having such a good time listening to Marvin answer questions that she forgot all about her vision—until Rocky splashed into the front hallway and stopped behind the massive turtle.

"Hey, Kiki," Rocky shouted. "There wasn't any gift for Marvin in Mr. Fangtooth's office."

Rocky's loud shouts startled Marvin and he jumped up high. His head whacked the huge chandelier, and the glowing jellyfish flew off, several plopping onto Mrs. Karp's head. *Plop! Plop! Plop!*

The chandelier's chain pulled loose from the ceiling of the large shell. Directly underneath the falling light was Rocky. He screamed and Marvin fell on top of Rocky, swirling and churning the water with thousands of bubbles. It was just like in Kiki's vision!

It was all happening so fast, no one knew what to do or how to help.

But suddenly the bubbles cleared, and everyone saw Marvin's body was curved over Rocky, *protecting* him! And there was Madame Hippocampus, who was above Marvin, holding the tremendous chandelier with her hooves.

"A little help here?" Madame Hippocampus called. Marvin moved from Rocky, and with Mrs. Karp's help Madame fastened the large light fixture back to the shell's ceiling.

Rocky was so scared, he hadn't moved a fin. His mouth was wide open.

Shelly, Echo, and Kiki swam over to him.

"Are you okay, Rocky? Can you move?" Kiki asked.

Rocky got up slowly. "That was awesome!" he said. "I wasn't scared one barnacle bit."

The three merfriends exchanged looks, not sure if Rocky was really telling the truth.

Kiki floated up to Madame Hippocampus. "Madame, what are you doing here?"

"I knew you were concerned about what you saw, and I wanted to be here—just in case. I didn't tell you the other day that I, too, have visions, but I didn't see this coming," Madame said. Then she smiled. "You're not alone, my dear."

Kiki smiled back and hugged her merology teacher. "Thank you so much."

Madame winked and swam away. "Visionaries have to stick together."

After Madame left, Marvin said it was also time for him to return home. "It's been a most exciting visit, mergirls and merboys. Thank you for inviting me. I hope to see you again one day."

And with that, the leatherback moved his huge body through the Trident Academy doors and swam off.

And in the next second, Rocky zoomed up beside Kiki and snapped, "What was the big idea? Why did you trick me?"

Shelly looked at Kiki. "That's what you get for trying to help him."

Kiki giggled. She was glad Rocky was all right, even if he was mad at her.

"Mrs. Karp, Kiki fibbed to me!" Rocky complained as he swam over to their teacher.

"Let me know if you have any dreams of Rocky moving away," Shelly said.

Kiki took a deep breath and smiled. "Guess what? I just had another vision."

"Really?" Echo asked. "Was it about Rocky?"

Kiki shook her head. "No, it was about us: that we'll be friends for a long, long time."

Shelly laughed. "See, we told you that visions are a good thing."

Kiki grinned. Maybe seeing the future could come in handy. She would have to wait and see.

Class Projects

Shelly and Wanda's House

SHELLY'S INTERVIEW QUESTION FOR MARVIN:

Why are you called "leatherback"?

MARVIN'S ANSWER: Instead of having a hard shell, I have a rubbery carapace that some think is leathery-looking.

WANDA'S INTERVIEW QUESTION FOR MARVIN:

If you don't have a shell, where do you hide your head?

MARVIN'S ANSWER: I've heard that some turtles can retract, or hide, their head, but leatherback turtles can't.

Echo and Rocky's House

ECHO'S INTERVIEW QUESTION FOR MARVIN:

Have you ever seen a human?

MARVIN'S ANSWER: Once I was caught in a human's fishing net. I thought I would die, but luckily a human man got me out. I pretended to be dead until he untangled me and then I jumped off his boat as fast as I could.

ROCKY'S INTERVIEW QUESTION FOR MARVIN: How many different kinds of turtles are there?

MARVIN'S ANSWER: There are seven species of sea turtles: Kemp's ridley, olive ridley, loggerhead, hawksbill, flatback, green, and leatherback. I've heard there are more on land.

Pearl and Kiki's House

PEARL'S INTERVIEW QUESTION FOR MARVIN:

How long can you stay underwater?

MARVIN'S ANSWER: The longest I've stayed under is eighty-five minutes.

KIKI'S INTERVIEW QUESTION FOR MARVIN:

Have you ever hurt a merkid?

MARVIN'S ANSWER: No, but I am a wild creature and weigh around two thousand pounds. No merkids or humans should come very close, for everyone's safety.

The Mermaid Tales Song

REFRAIN:

Let the water roar

Deep down we're swimming along

Twirling, swirling, singing the mermaid song.

VERSE 1:

Shelly flips her tail

Racing, diving, chasing a whale

Twirling, swirling, singing the mermaid song.

VERSE 2:

Pearl likes to shine

Oh my Neptune, she looks so fine

Twirling, swirling, singing the mermaid song.

VERSE 3:

Shining Echo flips her tail

Backward and forward without fail

Twirling, swirling, singing the mermaid song.

VERSE 4:

Amazing Kiki

Far from home and floating so free

Twirling, swirling, singing the mermaid song.

Author's Note

WHEN I WRITE A STORY, I do research. For *Mermaid Tales*, I study legends about mermaids, but I also learn about ocean creatures. I was sad to find out that many leatherback turtles die from eating plastic bags. The bags somehow get into the ocean, and the turtles eat them, thinking they are jellyfish. In fact, the International Union for the Conservation of Nature and Natural Resources lists the leatherback as "critically endangered" (facing an extremely high risk of extinction in the wild in the immediate future). One way to help turtles is to use cloth bags instead of plastic. I'm going to try to always use cloth bags for my groceries. I hope you'll join me. Together we can spread the word to save the leatherback!

Swim free,
Debbie Dadey

Glossary

CLEANER WRASSE: This little silvery-blue fish spends its whole life cleaning other fish, turtles, and sometimes even divers.

CLOWN FISH: If you have ever seen the movie *Finding Nemo*, you know that Nemo was a clown fish. This brightly colored fish is able to live among anemones. Other fish are stung by the anemones' tentacles, but not the clown fish.

GRAY HERON: This bird lives near water in

Europe, Asia, Japan, Indonesia, Africa, and Madagascar.

HUMPBACK WHALE: Humpbacks are the acrobats of the ocean, breaching (jumping out of the ocean) and slapping the water with their tales.

KILLER WHALE: Killer whales, or orcas, are known for their black and white markings. They are the largest member of the dolphin family.

LEATHERBACK TURTLE: Leatherback turtles' backs are flexible and rubbery.

MANTA RAY: The manta ray is the largest ray, but it is usually harmless to people. The southern stingray's venom causes severe pain.

MAUVE STINGER JELLYFISH: This stinging

jellyfish makes a light show when its mucus (snot) glows.

MOLLUSKS: This group of marine animals includes oysters, octopuses, and sea slugs.

MOTHER-OF-PEARL: This is the hard inner layer of the shell of a pearl oyster.

PEARLS: Pearls are often used in jewelry. They are made when oysters coat a grain of sand with a substance called nacre.

PORCUPINE FISH: When this fish is scared, it pumps water into its body and looks like a prickly soccer ball.

RIBBON EEL: The ribbon eel is black with a yellow fin when it is young, and changes to bright blue with a yellow snout as it gets older. Later in life it turns yellow.

SAILOR'S EYEBALL: This type of seaweed looks like a dark green marble.

SEA GRAPES: This is a kind of seaweed that has round sacs that look very much like grapes.

SEA LETTUCE: Animals and humans alike eat this plant that grows on seashores and in shallow waters.

SEA SQUIRT: This animal resembles a blob of green jelly.

SEAL: The common seal, or harbor seal, lives in the North Pacific and North Atlantic.

SEAWEED: Spectacular seaweed usually grows in very deep water. This type of seaweed is purple-blue when it is young.

SHARK: The sand tiger shark looks very scary

with its sharp teeth, but it is actually quite peaceful and is often used in aquariums.

SHELL: If you find a spiral shell on the beach, it probably belonged to a slug or snail. The shells protect their soft bodies.

SHRIMP AND KRILL: These creatures are relatives of crabs and lobsters.

STARFISH: Most starfish are bottom dwellers. While starfish usually have just five arms, there is a seven-arm starfish too.

TUBE SPONGE: This sponge is pinkish violet and often grows as bunches of tubes that are joined at the bottom.

FIND OUT WHAT HAPPENS IN THE NEXT . . .

Mermaid Tales

★ Debbie Dadey ★

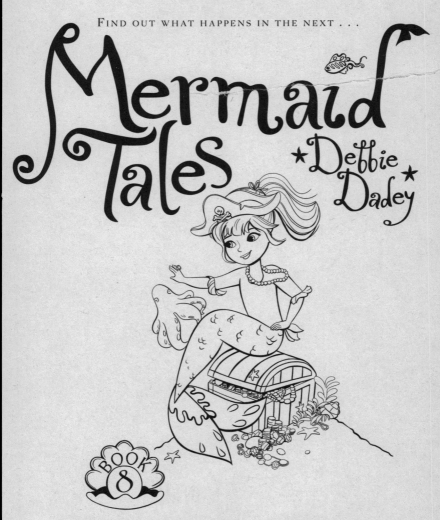

BOOK 8

Treasure in Trident City

Mirror, Mirror

PEARL SWAMP CURLED THE tip of her gold tail to make a bow. Then she flipped it out quickly to make a circle. It was hard to do while seated, but just for fun, she began practicing her Tail Flippers dance. Her school, Trident Academy, had a dance and gymnastics group called the Tail Flippers. Pearl was so proud that she'd made the team this year!

"Pearl!" her third-grade teacher, Mrs. Karp, snapped. "Are you paying attention?"

Pearl sat up straight and stared innocently at her teacher. "Of course! I always pay attention to you, Mrs. Karp." That wasn't *exactly* true. Pearl did *try* to pay attention, but sometimes school was just too boring! She longed for something exciting to happen.

"As I was saying, class," Mrs. Karp continued, "today we will start a storytelling project."

A merboy named Rocky Ridge groaned loud enough for the whole class to hear.

Pearl felt like groaning too. Mrs. Karp was always coming up with new projects for them, many of them very dull!

Mrs. Karp frowned at Rocky. "The project will include two assignments. For the first assignment, each of you will choose a story to study. Then you will practice telling it to your family or in front of a mirror. You will share your story with the class tomorrow."

Kiki Coral raised her hand. "What's a mirror?"

"Don't you have a mirror?" Pearl asked in surprise. Even though Kiki was from far-off waters, Pearl couldn't believe she didn't know what a mirror was!

Kiki shook her head. Most of the other

third graders shrugged, so Shelly Siren explained, "It's a piece of glass that you look in to see yourself. What you see is called a reflection. A lot of humans have them."

Pearl sniffed, tossing her long blond hair behind her shoulders. Shelly was such a know-it-all. Just because she lived with her grandfather in an apartment above the People Museum, she thought she was an expert on *all* human things. "My family has ten of them," Pearl bragged.

"No one has ten mirrors in their shell," Rocky scoffed.

Pearl lifted her pointy nose up in the water. "Well, *we* do! If you don't believe me, you can come over and see for yourself!"

Rocky made a face. "A giant octopus couldn't drag me to your shell."

"That's quite enough," Mrs. Karp said sharply. "If you don't have a mirror, you may practice with a friend."

A mergirl named Echo Reef raised her hand and asked, "What's the second part of the storytelling project?"

Mrs. Karp peered over her glasses and smiled at Echo. "Thank you for asking. The second assignment will be to make up your own story and tell it to the class."

"That's more like it." Rocky grinned, sitting back in his shell seat. "I'm good at making up stories."

Pearl knew that was true. Rocky was always making up tales, and they were usually great big fat lies. But even Pearl had to admit she liked the idea of being in front of the class and telling a story she made up. She could say almost anything! Plus, Pearl loved it when everyone was looking at her. It made her feel so special.

Mrs. Karp thumped her white tail on her desk to get everyone's attention. "It's time to head to the library to choose the stories for your first assignment." The merkids floated down the hall. Pearl wasn't eager to find a story among all the rock and seaweed books, but she did love looking at the beautiful, domed library ceiling. It was made of glistening mother-of-pearl, and its fancy chandeliers sparkled with glowing jellyfish. If the whole school was as pretty as the library, Pearl was sure she would like studying more.

Pearl and her friend Wanda Slug sat down at a rock table that was piled high with stories written on pieces of sea-weed. "What kind of story do you want to find?" Wanda asked. "I'd love one about a princess!"

Pearl scrunched her nose. "A princess would be all right, I guess," she said. "But only if it's *really* exciting."

Just then there was a loud yelp across the room. "No wavy way!" Rocky yelled. "Look what I found!"

Story Time!

ALMOST THE ENTIRE CLASS gathered around Rocky. "I found a story about a pirate treasure!" he exclaimed.

"Pirates are cool," a boy named Adam said, peering over Rocky's shoulder.

"That's not even the best part!" Rocky

boasted. "The treasure is right here in Trident City!"

Pearl floated over to Rocky as the other merkids giggled in excitement. After all, Trident Academy was located in the middle of Trident City. The treasure couldn't be too far away.

"It's just a pretend story from a book," Shelly said. "There's not really a treasure."

"But what if it's not made up?" Rocky protested. "What if it's real?"

Pearl squeezed in next to Rocky. Her eyes grew wide as she scanned the story, which included a faded drawing of an old, abandoned pirate ship. "It says there are diamonds as big as a merman's fist and rubies large enough to choke a shark!"

Rocky nodded. "And they're all hidden inside a treasure chest that's haunted by pirate ghosts."

"Ghosts?" Echo Reef shuddered. "Ghosts are creepy."

Shelly shook her head. "Ghosts aren't real."

Rocky pointed his brown tail at Shelly. "How do you know?"

"Yeah," Pearl said, rolling her big green eyes. "Ghosts are supposed to be invisible. For all you know, they're swimming all over this library." Pearl didn't believe in ghosts, but she hated when Shelly acted like she knew everything.

Echo looked around as if she expected a ghost to jump out at any moment.

"I know," Shelly said. "I just don't believe in them."

"Who cares about pirates or ghosts, anyway?" Pearl said. "I want to know where to find that treasure!"

Rocky continued to read the story aloud. "This doesn't say exactly where the treasure is, but you wouldn't want to go near it. The pirate ghosts guard it! There's no telling what they'd do to you if you tried to take it."

Just then the librarian, Miss Scylla, swam over with one eyebrow raised. "What's all the fuss about? Have you finished choosing your stories?" Everyone sighed and got back to work.

But Pearl couldn't stop thinking about

how thrilling it would be to find a real pirate's treasure. She'd probably even get her picture in the *Trident City Tide*, the local newsweed. She closed her eyes, imagining the headline: BEAUTIFUL YOUNG MERMAID FINDS TREASURE.

THAT NIGHT AT DINNER, PEARL ASKED her parents if they'd heard about the treasure in Trident City. "That's just a silly old legend," Mrs. Swamp said, wiping her mouth with a napkin.

"Actually," began Mr. Swamp, setting his glass of comb jelly tea on the marble table, "I've seen the ship. It's beyond Whale Mountain and the Big Volcano." Whale Mountain was a big underwater mountain shaped like the hump on a whale's back.

Pearl slapped the table gleefully. "I knew it!" She couldn't wait to tell that know-it-all Shelly that the treasure *was* real.

"But the ship is haunted," her dad said in a quiet voice.

Her mom laughed. "Don't be silly! There's no such thing as a haunted ship."

Her dad raised his eyebrows, picking up his glass. "Maybe not, but there's something spooky about that ship. Frank at work told me he swam by there one day and heard ghosts moaning. He said that over the years many merpeople have disappeared into that ship and have never been seen again."

Pearl's mom sighed. "You know Frank likes to make things up."

"It doesn't matter," Pearl's father said. "Merfolk stay away from it anyway, because the ship's wood is rotting. It's so old that the whole place is dangerous."

Pearl nodded and took another sip of her cuttlefish chowder. All she could think about was a big treasure chest full of diamonds and rubies.

Debbie Dadey

is the author and coauthor of more than one hundred and fifty children's books, including the series The Adventures of the Bailey School Kids. A former teacher and librarian, Debbie now lives in Bucks County, Pennsylvania, with her wonderful husband, three children, and three dogs. She recently went to Jamaica and thought she saw a mermaid there! If you see any mermaids, let her know at www.debbiedadey.com.

Candy Fairies

| Chocolate Dreams | Rainbow Swirl | Caramel Moon | Cool Mint | Magic Hearts |

| Gooey Goblins | The Sugar Ball | A Valentine's Surprise | Bubble Gum Rescue | Double Dip |

| Jelly Bean Jumble | The Chocolate Rose | A Royal Wedding | Marshmallow Mystery |

Visit
candyfairies.com
for more delicious
fun with your
favorite fairies.

Play games, download activities, and so much more!